A Sesame Street Start-to-Read Book™

Grover Goes to School

by Dan Elliott

illustrated by Normand Chartier

Featuring Jim Henson's Sesame Street Muppets

Random House/Children's Television Workshop

Library of Congress Cataloging in Publication Data:
Elliott, Dan. Grover goes to school. (Sesame Street start-to-read books). SUMMARY: On the first day of
school, Grover tries to please everyone but himself in order to make new friends. [1. School stories. 2. Friend-
ship—Fiction] I. Chartier, Normand, 1945-   ill. II. Title. III. Series. PZ7.E446Gr [E] 81-15398 AACR2
ISBN: 0-394-85176-5 (trade); 0-394-95176-X (lib. bdg.) Manufactured in the United States of America
5 6 7 8 9 0

Today was the big day.
It was the first day of school
for Grover!
And Grover was ready
before the sun came up.

His mother gave him
a brand-new pencil box,
a new box of big crayons,
a lunch box full of jelly sandwiches,
and a big hug and kiss good-bye.

"I will be the only one
from Sesame Street," said Grover.
"What if nobody likes me?"
His mother smiled. "Just be yourself,"
she said. "You are very lovable."

But Grover was not so sure.
He walked slowly to school.
"I will try hard to make
everyone like me," he said.

At school the teacher gave
all the children a big hello.
"My name is Mister Lester," he said.
"And what are your names?"

One by one they said their names.
"Truman!" "Jill!" "Molly!" "Bill!"
"Oh," said Grover to himself.
"There are SO many children!"

Finally it was Grover's turn.
He stood up and said shyly,
"I am Grover. I want to be
friends with everybody!"

After they all said their names,
Mister Lester let them draw pictures.
He passed out paper and
boxes of old crayons.
"I can use my own new crayons!"
said Grover.

Truman looked at Grover's crayons.
"Hey, Grover," said Truman,
"if you will give me your crayons,
    I will give you my truck."

Grover looked at the toy truck.

It was missing three wheels.

And Grover loved his new crayons!

"Oh, dear!" Grover said to himself.

"If I say no, Truman will not like me."

So he gave his crayons to Truman
and tried to play with the truck.
Bumpity-bump-bump went the truck.
It was not much fun.

Soon Mister Lester said,
"Time for milk and cookies!
But before you eat,
you must clean up!"

Then Grover had an idea.
"You can eat right now,"
  he said to the children near him.
"I, Grover the Cleaner-upper,
  will put everything away."
The children ran to the cookies.
"Thanks, Grover!" they shouted.

Grover cleaned up the crayons,
the lumps of green clay,
and the blocks on the floor.
"Now I will get my cookie,"
said Grover happily.

But all the cookies were gone.
"Oh, no! We forgot to save a cookie
for Grover!" the children said.
"It is okay. I do not mind,"
said Grover sadly.

Soon it was time to play outside.
"I will ask my new friends
to play hopscotch with me,"
said Grover.

But they were already jumping rope.
"You can turn the rope for us,"
said Jill.
Grover did not want to turn the rope. . . .
But he said, "Okay."

Finally it was time for lunch.
Grover opened his lunch box.
Truman watched him.
"If you give me your jelly sandwich,
I'll give you my baloney," said Truman.

Grover did not like baloney. . . .
But he said, "Okay."
Suddenly tears began rolling
down Grover's furry face.

"Why are you crying, Grover?"
asked Molly.

"Because," cried Grover,
"I do not like this broken truck.
I miss my crayons.
I did not get a cookie.
I do not like jump rope.
And I HATE BALONEY!"

Grover cried and cried.

"I will cheer you up," said Molly.

"Do you want to play marbles?"

Grover stopped crying.

"Well . . . I like jacks better,"
he said.

"I do not know how to play jacks,"
said Molly.
Grover started to cry again.

"But maybe you can teach me jacks,"
said Molly.

Now Grover really stopped crying.

"Oh, yes! I am SO happy to teach you!"
And he really meant it.

Molly got up to "threesies."
Then it was time to put away
the jacks and learn to write.

Grover opened his new pencil box.
"What a neat pencil box," said Bill.
"Want to trade?"

Grover looked at Bill's pencil box
and then at his own.
He thought for a minute.
Then Grover shook his head.
"No," he said. "I like mine better."

"Okay," said Bill.

And he was not mad!

Grover was so happy!

He smiled at Bill.

"Do you like jacks?" asked Grover.

"My favorite game!" said Bill.

"Mine, too!" said Grover.

After school Grover, Bill,
and Molly played jacks.
Then Grover ran home.
"I have two new friends!"
he told his mother.

"TWO new friends in ONE day,"
she said. "That is a lot!"
"It sure is!" said Grover.